There Was a Young Rabbi

A Hanukkah Tale

KAR-BEN PUBLISHING, INC.
An imprint of Lerner Publishing Group, Inc.
241 First Avenue North
Minneapolis, MN 55401 USA
1-800-4-KARBEN

Website address: www.karben.com

Main body text set in Amasis MT Std
Typeface provided by Monotype Typography

Library of Congress Cataloging-in-Publication Data

Names: Wolfe, Suzanne, 1949– author. | Ebbeler, Jeffrey, illustrator.
Title: There was a young rabbi : a Hanukkah tale / Suzanne Wolfe ; illustrated
by Jeffrey Ebbeler.
Description: Minneapolis : Kar-Ben Publishing, [2020] | Audience: Ages
   4–9. | Audience: Grades K–1. | Summary: "Hanukkah is a very busy time!
   Join the rabbi as she makes festive preparations — spinning the dreidel,
   cooking a tasty meal, lighting the menorah and more — in this cumulative,
   rhyming story to remember the miracle from a long time ago!"— Provided
   by publisher.
Identifiers: LCCN 2019043069 (print) | LCCN 2019043070
   (ebook) | ISBN 9781541576070 (library binding) | ISBN 9781541576087
   (paperback) | ISBN 9781541599536 (ebook)
Subjects: CYAC: Stories in rhyme. | Hanukkah—Fiction. | Rabbis—Fiction.
Classification: LCC PZ8.3.W8428 Th 2020 (print) | LCC PZ8.3.W8428
   (ebook) | DDC [E]—dc23

LC record available at https://lccn.loc.gov/2019043069
LC ebook record available at https://lccn.loc.gov/2019043070

Manufactured in the United States of America
1-46597-47602-1/3/2020

There Was a Young Rabbi

A Hanukkah Tale

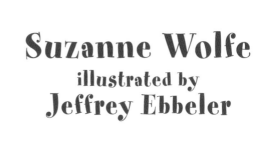

Suzanne Wolfe

illustrated by
Jeffrey Ebbeler

KAR-BEN
PUBLISHING

There was a young rabbi who read from the Torah. She read from the Torah and lit the menorah.

The story of Hanukkah does not appear in the Torah, but the Torah is read during this holiday.

She lit the menorah,
as we all know,
to remember a miracle
from a long time ago.

There was a young rabbi
who made latkes so yummy.
She fried them in oil,
then filled up her tummy.
She made latkes so yummy
and filled up her tummy.
She read from the Torah
and lit the menorah.

She lit the menorah,
as we all know,
to remember a miracle
from a long time ago.

There was a young rabbi
who made applesauce sweet.
She ate it with latkes
for a Hanukkah treat.
She ate applesauce sweet
for a Hanukkah treat.
She made latkes yummy
and filled up her tummy.

She read from the Torah
and lit the menorah.
She lit the menorah,
as we all know,
to remember a miracle
from a long time ago.

There was a young rabbi
who made a nice brisket.
It's kosher, of course,
or she wouldn't risk it!
Kosher brisket she made.
At least ten pounds it weighed.
She made applesauce sweet
for a Hanukkah treat.

She made latkes yummy
and filled up her tummy.
She read from the Torah
and lit the menorah.
She lit the menorah,
as we all know,
to remember a miracle
from a long time ago.

There was a young rabbi
who played dreidel to win.
She watched it closely
as it started to spin.

The dreidel — it spun.
The rabbi — she won!
Kosher brisket she made.
At least ten pounds it weighed.

She made applesauce sweet
for a Hanukkah treat.
She made latkes yummy
and filled up her tummy.
She read from the Torah
and lit the menorah.
She lit the menorah,
as we all know,
to remember a miracle
from a long time ago.

The menorah in the ancient temple had seven branches instead of the nine we have today.

There was a young rabbi
who ate chocolate gelt.
So sweet and so tasty,
in her mouth it did melt.
She ate chocolate gelt.
In her mouth it did melt.
The dreidel — it spun.
The rabbi — she won!

Kosher brisket she made.
At least ten pounds it weighed.
She made applesauce sweet
for a Hanukkah treat.

She made latkes yummy
and filled up her tummy.
She read from the Torah
and lit the menorah.
She lit the menorah,
as we all know,
to remember a miracle
from a long time ago.

There was a young rabbi,
and for eight straight nights,
she celebrated Hanukkah —
the Festival of Lights!
For eight straight nights,
the Festival of Lights!
She ate chocolate gelt.
In her mouth it did melt.

The dreidel — it spun.
The rabbi — she won!
Kosher brisket she made.
At least ten pounds it weighed.
She made applesauce sweet
for a Hanukkah treat.
She made latkes yummy
and filled up her tummy.
She read from the Torah
and lit the menorah.
She lit the menorah,
as we all know,
to remember a miracle
from a long time ago.

About Hanukkah

Hanukkah is an eight-day Festival of Lights that celebrates the victory of the Maccabees over the mighty armies of Syrian King Antiochus. According to legend, when the Maccabees came to restore the Holy Temple in Jerusalem, they found one jug of pure oil, enough to keep the menorah lit for just one day. But a miracle happened, and the oil burned for eight days. On each night of the holiday, we add an additional candle to the menorah, play the game of dreidel, and eat potato latkes fried in oil to remember this victory for religious freedom.

About the Author

Suzanne Wolfe is a retired teacher. A graduate of the University of Central Arkansas in Conway, Arkansas, she taught for over 34 years in public schools in Oklahoma and Texas. She lives in Oklahoma. This is her first children's book.

About the Illustrator

Jeffrey Ebbeler lectures in schools, colleges, and museums about the process of bringing words to life through pictures. He lives in Cincinnati with his wife and twin daughters. His previous books include *Lights Out Shabbat*.